# THE ESCAPADES OF CLINT McCOOL

## SOL-RAY MAN AND THE FREAKY FLOOD

*by Jane Kelley*
*illustrated by Jessika von Innerebner*

*Grosset & Dunlap*
*An Imprint of Penguin Random House*

GROSSET & DUNLAP
Penguin Young Readers Group
An Imprint of Penguin Random House LLC

Text copyright © 2017 by Jane Kelley. Illustrations copyright © 2017 by Penguin Random House LLC. All rights reserved. Published by Grosset & Dunlap, an imprint of Penguin Random House LLC, 345 Hudson Street, New York, New York 10014. GROSSET & DUNLAP is a trademark of Penguin Random House LLC. Manufactured in China.

*Library of Congress Cataloging-in-Publication Data is available.*

ISBN 9780451533395 (paperback)          10 9 8 7 6 5 4 3 2 1
ISBN 9780451533401 (library binding)     10 9 8 7 6 5 4 3 2 1

For my husband, Lee, whose great ideas always save the day—JK

To all the superheroes of the world, especially those who don't wear capes—JVI

# I NeeD My CAP

**My cap has a** Speed Accelerator button. Should I push it? Mom hates when flames shoot out of my shoes. Even pretend ones. Clint McCool doesn't need those rocket engines, anyway. I have fast feet.

*Varrrrooooom!* I fly down the stairs!
*Varrrrooooom!* I rush outside!
Oh no. Turtles are on the sidewalk!

*Screeeech!* I put on the brakes.

Hmm. Can I run on top of their shells? Nope. These aren't real turtles. They're kids with big backpacks. They walk so slow. Did they forget? Today Sol-Ray Man is coming to our school!

Sol-Ray Man is the most super superhero ever. He uses the sun's rays

to power up. He zooms to the disaster.
He activates his light beams. He
saves the planet three times in every
episode. And today he's going to tell
me how.

I zigzag around the turtles.

"Wait for me, Walter!" Mom yells.

That's right. She called me Walter.

She *named* me Walter after my grandpa. What a disaster! Luckily, I knew what to do. I named myself. Clint McCool.

"Hi, Clint McCool!" Marco shouts. He's at the corner with his mom.

I run up to him. He's the best Best Friend ever. He always calls me by my real name. He's supersmart. He made the buttons that control my powers. He tied each one to my cap. They help me save the day. That happens more than you'd think.

"Let's go, Marco! Sol-Ray Man is coming today!" I say.

"I know. Look what I made." Marco shows me his arms. He has special bands on his wrists. Each band has three shiny panels.

"Wow!" I say.

"XL7 Ray Benders," Marco says. "Sol-Ray Man uses them. They direct his beams."

"They *zap* around corners. *Zap* over buildings," I say. "*Zap* past his

archenemy Eclipse. So he can't block Sol-Ray Man's light," I say. "Let me see them work."

Marco doesn't take them off.

He moves his arm. Light zaps off the panels.

"Can I wear them?" I ask. "I need to show Sol-Ray Man I'm a superhero, too. I don't want him to think I'm just a kid."

"But, Clint McCool, you are a kid," Marco says.

I sigh. I know. Real life is so boring. Except when we can have an escapade. Or when my friend makes cool stuff that he should share. "Please, Marco?"

"You have your cap," Marco says.

"I can't wear my cap in school." Our teacher, Ms. Apple, always locks it in her desk. That's a mistake. I need the cap. It helps me focus. Then I can control my powers. Ms. Apple doesn't understand that. She's a grown-up.

"I probably can't wear these, either," Marco says.

Marco's right. School means rules. "Too bad we can't *zap* around the rules."

Then . . . *Zing, zong, zing.* Brain flash!

"I don't need my cap. I don't need all my powers—just one. And one button."

Hmmm. Which one should I choose? Invisibility? Idea Generator? Speed Accelerator? That's the one. Then I can race Sol-Ray Man around the auditorium.

I tug at the Speed Accelerator button. "Help me get it off."

Marco twists.

I yank. "Why did you tie it so tight?" I say.

"So you wouldn't lose it," Marco says.

"What are you guys doing?" M.L. comes over to us. She's our best friend, too. She can walk on her hands. For real. She doesn't even have to cheat.

"Tug of war? I can beat you both," M.L. says.

She could do it, too. She's superstrong.

"Maybe later," I say. "I need this Speed Accelerator button."

M.L. grabs the button. Marco and I hold the cap. She pulls.

*Pop!* The string breaks. The button comes off. It flies through the air.

"Catch it!" Marco says.

I push the Jump button on my cap. I *boing* really high. But not high enough.

The Speed Accelerator button lands in the gutter. It rolls down through the grate. Disaster!

# 2

# A ReAL DiSASTER ?

"*Get that button!*" I kneel in the gutter. I stick my hand between the metal bars. I wiggle my fingers. "I can't reach it."

"Maybe I can lift the grate." M.L. tugs at the bars. They don't move.

Marco makes a fish hook out of a paper clip. "Let me try." He catches some slimy leaves.

Big hands come down from the sky and pull us up. Is it monsters? No, just moms.

"I need my button," I say.

"Stay away from the alligators," Mom says.

"Are there alligators under the street?" I ask.

Our moms laugh. *Heh heh heh heh.*
What's so funny? I push my
Translator button. It usually helps me
understand grown-ups. But today I
don't get English. I get Italian. "Salami
pizza?"

"Some people think alligators live
in the underground pipes," Marco's
mom says.

"They do?" I say.

"They're wrong," M.L.'s mom says.

I look between the bars. I see something shiny. Is it a button? Or an alligator's eye? This could be an escapade. If only our moms weren't here.

"Come on, kids. You'll be late for school," M.L.'s mom says.

"Then we'll be late for work," Marco's mom says.

I stick my hand in again.

"Did you forget about Sol-Ray Man?" Mom asks.

Clint McCool never forgets! His brain just gets busy sometimes.

We all run to the school yard. M.L. lets me win. Our moms say good-bye.

Ms. Apple leads us into the school building.

We pass a poster on the wall. It's a picture of Sol-Ray Man. **USE YOUR LIGHT! POWER UP!**

I touch the empty space on my cap.

"I'm sorry," M.L. says. "I pulled too hard."

I sigh. I know I should say it's okay. But it isn't! "How will I ever be fast again?" I say.

"Don't worry, Clint McCool. You don't need that button," Marco says.

I look at his XL7 Ray Benders. "Maybe I could have something else?"

Marco pulls his sleeves down over the shiny panels.

"You're still a superhero," M.L. says.

M.L. is right. *Zing, zong, zing.* Brain flash! My cap has lots of buttons. I'll choose another one. What about the Jump button? If I can't go fast, then I could go high.

I push it. I jump around the classroom to practice. *Boing. Boing. Boing.*

Ms. Apple puts her hand on my head. I try to jump sideways. I can't.

"Walter. Give me the cap right now, or you can't go see Sol-Ray Man." Ms. Apple puts my cap in her desk. *Bang.* She slams the drawer shut.

*BANG!* A bigger noise comes from Thirteenth Street.

People shout from outside. Water gushes. It sounds like a million people are taking a shower. At the same time? That's impossible.

But the noises are real. They aren't something I made up in my head.

What's going on?

All the kids are at the window. I run to look. M.L. lifts me up so I can see.

A fountain of water shoots up from the street. It's taller than the trees. It's wider than a car. What is it?

"Everybody get back!" people yell. "Water main break!"

# 3

# ALLigATORS UNDERGROUND

**K**ids scream, "Whoa!"

Kids shout, "Wow!"

Where does the water come from? I see a big hole in Thirteenth Street.

"Who broke the street?" I ask.

"Water flows through pipes under the street," Ms. Apple says. "There's lots of pressure. If an old pipe breaks, the water shoots up through the hole."

Ms. Apple must be wrong. It can't be a hole in an old pipe. It's way too exciting.

"Everyone sit down," Ms. Apple says. "The workers will turn off the water and fix the pipe. They don't need our help."

"Yes they do!" I shout. "What about the alligators?"

"Our moms were just kidding, Clint McCool," Marco says.

"Moms never kid!" I say. "The alligators live in the pipes. They mostly sleep. But M.L. broke off my Speed Accelerator button. It went down the drain. It made one alligator superfast. He swam circles around the others."

Kids stare at me. I show them how an alligator swims.

"The other alligators got mad. They started a fight. Their tails thrashed."

I don't have a tail. I use my arm. I knock over a chair. M.L.'s lunch spills onto the floor.

"That's enough, Walter," Ms. Apple says.

"The tails break the pipes. Water whooshes out." I explode up from the ground. I don't spit water. That would be gross.

"The smartest alligator sees the hole. He thinks, 'Hey, I don't have to live in a sewer.' He crawls out of the pipe." I pull myself across my desk.

Ms. Apple drags my chair to the corner. She points to it. "Walter, sit down! Everyone take your seats!" Ms. Apple shouts. "Or I will give you all a test!"

Kids gasp. They scurry to their chairs. But blank spaces on paper don't scare me.

"I can't sit down. Water is gushing! Alligators are fighting! Somebody has to save the day!" I say. But how?

I need my cap. What button should I use? The Reverse Time-O-Meter? Then I could go back to before M.L. lost the button. Invisibility? Then I could sneak out of school and fight the alligators. How can I do that? I'll need help. M.L. is strong. Marco is smart. But alligators are big. And have lots of teeth. I sit down, but not to listen to Ms. Apple, I have to think.

*Zing, zong, zing.* Brain flash!

"We need Sol-Ray Man!"

I rush to the window.

I see fire trucks. I see police officers. I see barricades.

The spout of water is gone. Now there's a river on Thirteenth Street.

Where's Sol-Ray Man? He should be here by now. What happened? Did his archenemy Eclipse block his way?

Wait! I see Sol-Ray Man! On the other side of the river on Thirteenth Street.

I wave my arms. "Sol-Ray Man! Sol-Ray Man!"

"Attention, please. Attention, please." Principal Torres's voice crackles out of the speaker on the wall.

"There has been a water main break on Thirteenth Street. No one has been hurt. No one is in danger,"

Principal Torres says. "The workers must shut down our water. School will be closed."

"Yay!" Kids jump up and cheer.

Don't they realize what this means?

"What about the assembly?" I ask.

"What about Sol-Ray Man?"

"Your guardians have been called," Principal Torres says. "They will pick you up from the cafeteria. Classes will be dismissed one at a time. Wait for further instructions."

"Wait? Why do we have to wait?" I say. "Sol-Ray Man can save the day. He'll raise his arms to the sky. His XL7 Ray Benders will zap sunbeams to the street. The light will fix the pipe. And I will help him fight the alligators."

But none of that can happen.

Sol-Ray Man turns. He walks away from the river on Thirteenth Street. Away from the disaster. And away from me.

# 4

# WATCH OUT!
# ARCHENEMY!

*rush to the door.* Ms. Apple gets there first. Hmmm. Does she have superpowers, too?

"Wait for instructions, Walter," Ms. Apple says.

"Sol-Ray Man is leaving. I have to see him," I say.

"I'm sorry, Walter," Ms. Apple says. "Maybe Sol-Ray Man can come

another day."

"Another day?" I wail. That will be too late. He needs to tell me superhero stuff. Like how to fight enemies after bedtime. Do superheroes really eat spinach, or did Mom make that up? And the most important thing of all. Why did he leave? Why didn't he save the day?

*Rat-a-tat-tat-tat-tat.*

Oh no! Sol-Ray Man is being attacked.

I run to the window. I don't see any monsters.

*Rat-a-tat-tat-tat-tat-tat.*

"Marco, what's going on?" I ask.

"That's a jackhammer," Marco says.

"Jack Hammer! Is he Sol-Ray Man's new archenemy?"

"No, Clint McCool. Look." Marco points to a worker.

The worker leans on a machine shaped like a *T*. The point at the bottom breaks a hole in the cement.

"I knew that," I say. "I was just fooling."

Marco smiles.

"Why is he tearing up the street? There's already a hole," I say.

"The workers dig up the broken pipe. Then they put in a new one," Marco says.

I rush to Ms. Apple. "We don't need to leave. They're fixing it."

"It will take hours," Ms. Apple says. "Now gather up your belongings."

Kids grab their backpacks. M.L. unwraps the foil off her sandwich. She sneaks a bite. Everyone gets ready but me. I won't go home. I can't.

*Rat-a-tat-tat-tat-tat.*

I put my hands over my ears. The noise makes it hard to think.

I wish I had my Idea Generator. It's in Ms. Apple's desk. Could Marco make me another one?

I look at Marco. Sunbeams bounce off his XL7 Ray Benders.

*Zing, zong, zing.* Brain flash! Now I know what to do. I can help Sol-Ray Man save the day!

"*Pssst.* Marco."

"Be quiet, Walter," Ms. Apple says.

I shrug. I know I should ask Marco first. But I can't. Ms. Apple won't let me talk.

I crawl between the desks. I reach up. I grab one XL7 Ray Bender. I pull it off Marco's arm. I scurry back to my desk.

"Hey!" Marco says.

"Marco!" Ms. Apple says.

"Attention, please." Principal Torres talks through the speaker. "Your guardians are in the cafeteria. Kindergartners should go there now. Everyone else will wait."

Luckily, I don't have to pay attention to what she says. I can think about saving the day.

I put on the XL7 Ray Bender. It zaps a tiny sunbeam out the window.

Has the day been saved?

No. I shake my wrist. Hmmm. Maybe it needs a bigger panel? I look for supplies in my desk. I find lots of notes from Ms. Apple, three broken pencils, and a banana.

I need something shiny. But what?

The classroom only has books. Then I see M.L.'s sandwich. I grab it.

"Hey!" M.L. says.

I unwrap the foil. I push away the sandwich. It falls on the floor. That's okay. Now M.L. can pick it up. I stick the pencils in the wrist band. They fall over.

"*Pssst.* M.L. Do you have gum?" I whisper.

M.L. glares at me.

That's okay. I have some stored under my chair. I reach down to get it. I stick the gum on the wrist band. I stick the pencils in the gum. I stick the tinfoil on the pencils. My invention looks great. Now I have a super-duper XL7 Ray Bender!

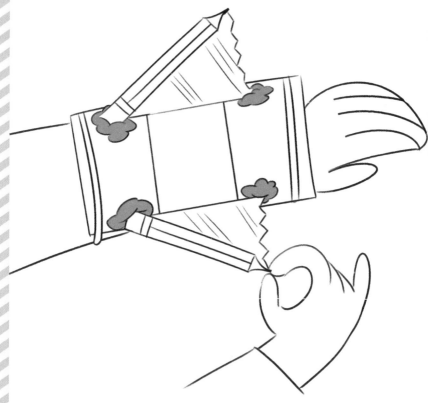

I raise my arm. It needs to be closer to the sun. I stand up.

"What did you do to my invention?" Marco says.

He looks mad. Hmmm. I wonder why. I just made it better.

Suddenly, a voice calls, "Yoo-hoo! Wally!"

"Wally?" all the kids say.

I forgot that there is a worse name than Walter.

An old woman staggers into the classroom. She wears a spotted raincoat and big boots. She carries an umbrella with ruffles. A plastic bag covers her hair. "There you are, Wally."

It's *my* archenemy—Mrs. Brussels.

# 5

# NoT MRs. BRusseLs!

"**O**h, *Wally!*" Mrs. Brussels wobbles over to me. She pretends to give me a hug. But she smothers me in her plastic coat. I fight my way out.

"I rushed right over the minute your mommy called," Mrs. Brussels says.

"Guardians are supposed to wait

in the cafeteria," Ms. Apple says.

"I'm Wally's babysitter," Mrs. Brussels says.

"Babysitter?" M.L. says.

Clint McCool is not a baby! I make a tough face.

Mrs. Brussels pats my cheek. "Have

you had a hard day? Soon you can curl up with Mr. Snuggles and take a nap."

"Mr. Snuggles?" M.L. says.

"That's

43

what Wally calls my fuzzy robe. He
holds it when he sucks his thumb,"
Mrs. Brussels says.

"I don't suck my thumb!" I shout.

"That's right, Wally. You don't,"

Mrs. Brussels says. "You chew your fingers."

Everyone is laughing. At me!

"Ms. Apple," says Principal Torres from the speaker. "Please lead your class to the cafeteria."

"Everyone follow me," Ms. Apple says. "Walter, you can go with Mrs. Brussels."

Ms. Apple gives my cap to Mrs. Brussels.

"Come along, Wally." Mrs. Brussels grabs my hand.

This is terrible! I break free from Mrs. Brussels. I rush over to Marco and M.L. I fly through the air. They step backward. I land on the floor. I grab their ankles.

"Please come with me," I say. I'm not ashamed to beg. "I'm not mad at you anymore."

"You're not mad at *us*?" Marco says.

"What did *we* do?" M.L. says.

"You lost my button down the drain. And you wouldn't share your XL7 Ray Benders," I say. I smile up at them. I wipe some slobber off their shoes.

M.L. puts her arm around Marco. They follow the other kids out of the classroom.

I call after them. "Don't you want to have an escapade?"

They don't even look at me.

The door shuts.

"My goodness, Wally. Those

children didn't even say good-bye," Mrs. Brussels says.

"They forgot," I say. I try to fix the XL7 Ray Bender. The extra foil falls on the floor. Everything is ruined.

*Zing, zong, zing.* Brain flash! I have to find Sol-Ray Man. Together we can fix the water pipe. After we save the day, Marco and M.L. will be so impressed. They'll have to be my friends again.

"Hurry up, Mrs. Brussels." I saw Sol-Ray Man walk away from the school. I have to catch up to him.

I try to drag Mrs. Brussels down the stairs. She holds the railing.

"No need to rush, Wally. Better safe than sorry," Mrs. Brussels says. "Remember when you fell down my steps? You got an owie on your knee. You cried and cried."

I'm not listening. She doesn't fool me. She wants me to be a baby. But she won't win.

We get to the first floor. She gasps for breath. I grab my cap. I put it on my head. I run out the front door. I hurry toward Thirteenth Street. I hear Jack Hammer. *Rat-a-tat-tat-tat-tat.*

Oh no! Big blue boards block the sidewalk. A river flows down Thirteenth Street. How can I follow Sol-Ray Man?

*Zing, zong, zing.* Brain flash! I can take the boards and make a raft!

I rush over to one board. I try to lift it up.

A guard grabs my arm. "What do you think you're doing?"

"I have to find Sol-Ray Man!" I say.

"Does this one belong to you?" the guard says to Mrs. Brussels.

"That's my Wally." Mrs. Brussels pinches my cheek.

"You can't cross here. You have to go to Fourteenth Street and go around the block," the guard says.

"But Sol-Ray Man and I need to save the day!" I say.

"Ha, ha, ha." Mrs. Brussels laughs. "Silly Wally. You'll do no such thing. It's time for your nap."

"Noooooo!" I shout. Is this the end? Has Clint McCool been defeated?

# 6

# SAVING THE DAY

**M**rs. Brussels hooks my arm with her umbrella. She drags me toward Fourteenth Street. "You need a nice rest. With Mr. Snuggles. After your nap, it will be lunchtime. I'll make creamed spinach. And for a treat, stewed prunes. Won't that be yummy in your tummy?"

My stomach groans, *No!*

I pat it. I promise it nachos and
sour gum balls and pepperoni pizza.
It's still upset.

We turn the corner. We walk up Fourteenth Street. We walk past the school.

I can't hear Jack Hammer anymore. I hear children shouting from the playground across the street.

They're having fun. I'm not. They're with their friends. I'm not. My friends didn't want to be with me. But I don't know why.

I push the Idea Generator button. I wait for a brain flash.

I don't get one. I push the button again. Nothing. I pound on it.

"Wally, my goodness. Is your hat bothering you? I can hold it," Mrs. Brussels says.

Mrs. Brussels grabs my cap. I hang on tight. We walk down the sidewalk together.

"Those buttons look so sharp. Don't worry. We'll make them nicer. I have soft pink yarn at home."

I groan. What's wrong with my cap? Did Mrs. Brussels deactivate it? I need to fix it. But how?

Marco would know. He knows everything. M.L. would help him. She helps everyone.

*Zing, zong, zing.* Brain flash!

"I need my friends!" I shout.

"But, Wally, sweetie pie, they didn't want to play with you," Mrs. Brussels says.

She's right. They didn't.

Hmm. I wonder why. Maybe because I wrecked their stuff and said bad things. Why was I so mean? They aren't my enemies.

Forget Sol-Ray Man! I need to find Marco and M.L. before another terrible thing can happen. We already had an alligator fight, a water pipe break, and a Mrs. Brussels attack. But the worst thing ever is no friends!

"When your mommy called, I was so happy," Mrs. Brussels says.

"Just think, we get to spend all day together."

I groan. We walk past the playground. Some preschool kids are playing in the sandbox. Grown-ups sit on benches close to Fourteenth Street.

"Aren't we lucky?" Mrs. Brussels says.

I don't feel lucky.

Then I hear Marco and M.L. laughing. They're up on the jungle gym.

I wave at them. They don't see me. I need to go to my friends.

Mrs. Brussels walks past the playground. Why is she going faster now? I have to stop her.

"What nice benches. Mrs. Brussels,

wouldn't you like to rest?" I say.

"Oh no," Mrs. Brussels says.

How can I make Mrs. Brussels stay? Can I bribe her? I don't have any creamed spinach. Or prunes. What else does she like? Besides telling embarrassing stories about me.

*Zing, zong, zing.* Brain flash!

Marco's mom is sitting on the bench. "Hi, Marco's mom. This is Mrs. Brussels. She's my babysitter," I say. "She changed my diapers."

"Oh yes. That was a job," Mrs. Brussels says. "One time, Wally's mom lost her ring. She thought Wally ate it. How could she get it back? Well. What

goes in must come out. So day after day, I had to keep a lookout."

Mrs. Brussels sits on the bench.

I rush over to Marco and M.L. I climb up on the jungle gym.

"I'm sorry," I say. "I shouldn't have stolen your XL7 Ray Bender. I shouldn't have messed up your sandwich. I shouldn't blame you when things go wrong. I shouldn't even blame Mrs. Brussels."

We look at her. She is still talking. The grown-ups are holding their noses. It's a terrible story.

"Maybe just a little?" M.L. says.

We all laugh and climb higher.

Marco fixes the messed-up XL7 Ray Bender. He gives it to me. I give it to

M.L. "Here. You wear it. I have my cap."

Marco and M.L. hold up their arms. "Let's zap a message to Sol-Ray Man," I say.

"Tell him Clint McCool wants to meet him," M.L. says.

Hmm. I wonder if that will work.

Then we hear a big noise from Thirteenth Street.

*CRASH!*

# 7

# MONSTERS?

"**W**hat was that?" I ask. We look across the playground toward Thirteenth Street. We don't see anything. Now we hear water gushing. Like someone flushed a giant toilet. We hear grown-ups shouting. "Stop digging! Another pipe broke!"

"Another pipe?" M.L. says.

The gushing sound gets louder.

"Look!" Marco says.

Water is coming from Thirteenth Street. It flows across the playground.

The little kids in the sandbox don't see it. They are too busy fighting over a shovel.

The grown-ups are sitting on the benches by Fourteenth Street. Mrs. Brussels is still talking. "Finally I found the ring."

The water comes closer to the little kids. It's brown and dirty. Old bottles and pieces of wood float by.

"Save the kids!" I shout.

M.L., Marco, and I climb down. We each grab a little kid. The kids

wriggle. They don't want to be picked
up. We carry them to the jungle gym.

We climb up the rungs just as the
water rushes under our feet.

Water flows across the sandbox.
The shovel floats toward the benches.

The grown-ups try to get their little kids. One lady slips and falls in the water.

Marco's mom helps her up. The grown-ups stand on the benches.

"Wally, what have you done now?"

Mrs. Brussels says. She opens her umbrella.

The little kids are scared. They reach toward the grown-ups. "I want Mommy!"

"Stay there! Stay there!" the grown-ups yell.

My kid wriggles free. I grab her waist.

M.L.'s kid tries to climb down. "I'm scared!" he says.

"Help!" M.L. shouts.

Marco tries to. But he has to hold onto his own kid. "Help!" Marco says.

We all need help.

"Mommy!" the little kids yell. They keep squirming.

"Don't leave. You have to help save the day!" I shout.

"How?" they wail.

I don't know how.

*Zing, zong, zing.* Brain flash! The kids need to do something. Then

they can be heroes.

"See the water? There are alligators down there," I say.

"Alligators!" the little kids shriek.

"Luckily they're in a cage," I say.

"What cage?" M.L. says.

"This one." I pat the bars of the jungle gym. "But we have to keep the cage from breaking apart. Everybody hold the bars. Tight. Squeeze them together!" I shout.

"Like this, Clint McCool?" Marco puts his kid's hands on the bar.

"Yes! Use both hands," I say.

The kids all squeeze the bars.

"Where are the alligators?" one kid asks.

"They're hiding. Don't worry. They

can't escape. If we keep the cage together," I say. "Oh, oh, M.L. You aren't using both hands."

M.L. puts her left hand back on the bar. "Like this, Clint McCool?"

"That's great," I say.

"I'm tired," one kid says.

"We need everybody to hold on tight. You can do it. You've got superpowers," I say.

"How do you know?" another kid asks.

"Because . . ." I look at Marco. "How do I know?"

"Because he's Clint McCool. He knows all about saving the day," Marco says.

I hear lots of splashing behind me.

Something big is coming toward us. What could it be?

Maybe there really are alligators. Maybe they want more buttons. Can alligators climb bars?

If the kids see the alligators, they'll get scared. They won't want to hang on. But they need to. Now more than ever.

"Look at your hands! Use your laser beam eyes! Give your muscles extra strength!"

*Splash, splash, splash.* It's getting closer.

Water splashes up against our legs.

Big hands grab me from behind.

Everybody screams!

# 8

# A Real Superhero

**S**omeone *tries* to pull me off the bars. I kick him away. I have to keep saving the kids.

"We got you," a firefighter says.

Three firefighters carry the little kids. Two police officers carry Marco and M.L.

A familiar voice says in my ear, "You can let go now."

I look over my shoulder.
Sol-Ray Man holds me.

I rub my eyes. I can't believe it. I know I imagined the alligators. Is he really real?

His cape floats in the breeze. His big hands hold me above the water. I touch his XL7 Ray Benders. They sparkle more than Marco's.

Sol-Ray Man carries me toward Fourteenth Street.

My brain is zinging and zonging. I need to calm down. I don't have a button that does that! I hold my cap on tight. That helps—a little.

I'm with Sol-Ray Man! I can talk to him! I have so much to say!

I open my mouth. "*Blub, blub, blub,*" comes out.

Oh no! I push the Translator

button. "Pasta, ziti," I say.

Italian again? I groan. Where are the words I need?

The firemen carry all the kids up Fourteenth Street. The grown-ups wait on dry ground.

Sol-Ray Man puts me down near them. Mrs. Brussels tries to smother me in her coat.

"What a flood," Mrs. Brussels says. "Just like when you put your whale slippers in the toilet."

I groan.

"Remember, Wally?" Mrs. Brussels asks. "Wally?"

Sol-Ray Man smiles. "Answer your grandma, Wally."

Disaster! Sol-Ray Man thinks I'm a

kid. How can I show him I'm not?

A news crew is on the street.

"Sol-Ray Man, can you tell us what happened?" a reporter asks. "You had to save the day for real. How come you were wearing your costume?"

"I usually wear jeans and a

T-shirt." Sol-Ray Man laughs. "I was supposed to talk to the schoolkids this morning. The water main broke. My talk got canceled. I was on my way home when the second pipe broke. The playground flooded. We had to save the kids."

"The water could have washed them away," the firefighter says. "Luckily, they were on the jungle gym."

"But they weren't. The preschoolers were in the sandbox," Marco's mom says.

"How did they get to safety?" the reporter asks.

"The big kids carried us," says one kid.

The reporter comes over to Marco, M.L., and me. "You did?"

"Everybody was scared. We didn't want to go. But Clint McCool knew what to do," says the second kid.

"He said we'd be okay if we held the bars. That kept the alligators in the cage," says the third kid.

"So we did," says the first kid.

"That was a good idea," the reporter says.

"How did you think of it?" M.L. asks.

"Did you push your Idea Generator button?" Marco points to it on my cap.

"What's that?" Sol-Ray Man says. "Can I see?"

I give my cap to Sol-Ray Man. He holds it. He carefully touches the buttons. I feel tingling all over.

"Is this where you get your superpowers?" Sol-Ray Man asks.

I can't speak. Not even Italian.

"That's how he activates them," Marco says. "He already has the powers."

"Let's get a photo of the two superheroes," the reporter says.

Sol-Ray Man kneels down by me. Now we're the same height. "Smile, Clint McCool," he says.

I'm already smiling. I'm so happy. Then I see Marco and M.L.

"Wait," I say. "Marco and M.L. need to be in the picture, too. And the kids."

"Everybody?" the reporter asks.

"Everybody. We're all superheroes," I say.

Mrs. Brussels pushes in front of me. "I better stand with my Wally."

Sol-Ray Man lifts me up. Marco and M.L. raise their arms. Their XL7 Ray Benders zap beams to the sky. The camera flashes.

"We all worked together!" I say. "That's how you really save the day!"

Check out Clint's first adventure:

# THE ESCAPADES OF
# CLINT McCOOL

## OCTO-MAN AND THE
## HEADLESS MONSTER